**To my high school writing teacher, Karal Baker Taylor,
who encouraged passion over perfection**

—B. O.

To Cole

—S. H.

MARGARET K. McELDERRY BOOKS

An imprint of Simon & Schuster Children's Publishing Division

1230 Avenue of the Americas, New York, New York 10020

Text copyright © 2018 by Barbara Odanaka

Illustrations copyright © 2018 by Sydney Hanson

MARGARET K. McELDERRY BOOKS is a trademark of Simon & Schuster, Inc.

For information about special discounts for bulk purchases, please contact Simon & Schuster Special Sales at 1-866-506-1949
or business@simonandschuster.com.

The Simon & Schuster Speakers Bureau can bring authors to your live event. For more information or to book an event, contact
the Simon & Schuster Speakers Bureau at 1-866-248-3049 or visit our website at www.simonspeakers.com.

Book design by Sonia Chaghatzbanian

The text for this book was set in VAG Rounded Std.

The illustrations for this book were rendered digitally.

Manufactured in China

0718 SCP

First Edition

2 4 6 8 10 9 7 5 3 1

Library of Congress Cataloging-in-Publication Data

Names: Odanaka, Barbara, author. | Hanson, Sydney, illustrator.

Title: Construction cat / Barbara Odanaka ; illustrated by Sydney Hanson.

Description: First Edition. | New York : Margaret K. McElderry Books, [2018] | Summary: After saying goodbye to her loving
family, a hard-working mother cat heads to her job at a construction site.

Identifiers: LCCN 2018006636 (print) | LCCN 2017061501 (eBook)

ISBN 9781481490948 (hardcover) | ISBN 9781481490955 (eBook)

Subjects: | CYAC: Stories in rhyme. | Cats—Fiction. | Construction workers—Fiction. | Families—Fiction.

Classification: LCC PZ8.3.O275 (print) | LCC PZ8.3.O275 Co 2018 (eBook) | DDC [E]—dc23

LC record available at https://lccn.loc.gov/2018006636

BARBARA ODANAKA · SYDNEY HANSON
CONSTRUCTION CAT

Margaret K. McElderry Books
New York London Toronto Sydney New Delhi

Construction Cat wakes up at dawn,

Grabs her boots
and tugs them on,

Buckles tool belt,
nice and snug,

Gives her family one more hug.

"Good-bye, good-bye!"
her kittens say.

A kiss for Pa, she's on her way.

Construction Cat drives her truck,
Bumpity-bump, through the muck.

Grabs her hard hat, greets the crew,
Rolls out blueprints to review.

"**Time to build!**" the workers say.
Tails high, they start their day.

Construction Cat begins to dig,
Shifting levers in the rig.

Whiskers twitching, eyes alert—
She's a whiz at moving dirt.

Construction Cat guides the crane,
Laying down the water main.
Concrete mixer starts to roar.

Lugging lumber, pounding nails,
Flicking sawdust from their tails,

Teams of cats, swift and strong,
Singing their construction song:

"Hammers! Shovels! Drills and saws!
"Handy tools for handy paws!
"Gulps of milk to quench our thirst!

"Watch your step. . . .
"SAFETY FIRST!"

The whistle blows; it's time for lunch.
Construction Cat begins to munch.
Carrots, crackers . . . oh, what's this?
A note from home!
Mother's bliss.

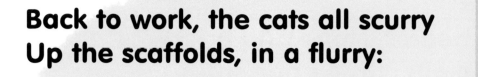

Back to work, the cats all scurry
Up the scaffolds, in a flurry:

Sawing, sanding—sweeping, too.
Clouds of dust—achoo, **achoo!**

Bamboo beams, stone and brick.
Hoisting walls, strong and thick.
Grind and scrape. Pound and pour.
"Come on, cats—one more floor!"

Construction Cat checks her list,
Making sure that nothing's missed.

"Okay, cats, just one more thing . . .

"A golden bell. . . .

"Let it ring."

Construction Cat packs up her gear.
Suddenly, a joyful cheer:

"Surprise! Surprise!" her kittens say.
A kiss from Pa . . .

A purrrrfect day.